For
Rory, Millie, Ella & Melody

Published in 2010 by Windmill Books, LLC
303 Park Avenue South, Suite # 1280, New York, NY 10010-3657

Adaptations to North American Edition © 2010 Windmill Books
Text copyright © 2004 Alan Bowater
Illustrations copyright © Pete Pascoe

Originally published by JoJo Publishing
"Yarra's Edge"
2203/80 Lorimer Street
Docklands VIC 3008
Australia

In conjunction with Purple Pig Productions

CREDITS:
Text by Alan Bowater
Illustrated by Pete Pascoe
Designed by Pete Pascoe, Alan Bowater, and Rob Ryan

Publisher Cataloging Data

Bowater, Alan
       A cat called Kitty. – North American ed. / written by Alan Bowater ; illustrated by Pete Pascoe.
              p.   cm. – (A pig called Pete)
       Summary: When Pete the flying pig meets Kitty from Kathmandu, they discover finding a friend is even better than flying
around the world.
              ISBN 978-1-60754-561-3 (lib.) – ISBN 978-1-60754-562-0 (pbk.)
ISBN 978-1-60754-563-7 (6-pack)
              1. Friendship—Juvenile fiction   2. Swine—Juvenile fiction   3. Cats—Juvenile fiction   [1. Friendship—Fiction
2. Pigs—Fiction   3. Cats—Fiction]   I. Pascoe, Pete   II. Title: Pig called Pete meets-- a cat called Kitty   III. Title   IV. Series
       [E]—dc22

Printed in the United States of America

For more great fiction and nonfiction, visit windmillbooks.com.

A Cat Called Kitty

Written by Alan Bowater

Illustrated by Pete Pascoe

alphabet

soup™

an imprint of

WINDMILL BOOKS™

New York

Every night my pig called Pete flies around the world.

"Just for fun," he grunts.

In Australia he rides a red kangaroo
with a didgeridoo.

In Tokyo he comes face-to-face
with a big sumo wrestler.

In Rome he "pigs" out on pizza and "slurpy" spaghetti.

In the sky above Paris he rides
a fast Jumbo Jet.

Under the Eiffel Tower he meets Kitty.

A cat called Kitty from Kathmandu!

She is fluffy white
and wears a feathery boa and a floppy hat.

In a sidewalk café they eat frogs' legs and snails!

They visit the Louvre and see Mona Lisa smile.

Pete tells Kitty he wants her to fly around the world with him.

The next morning they meet in the park for flying lessons.

Kitty flaps. Yes? No!

Kitty glides. Yes? No!

Kitty soars. Yes? No!

Kitty zooms. Yes? No!

Kitty hovers. Yes? No!

She just can't fly. Not one little bit!

Kitty is sad.

So is Pete, who flies back home.

I'm still awake.
The moonlight beams
through my bedroom
window.

"Hi, Pete." He doesn't answer.

In the morning I ask Pete, "What's wrong?"
He tells me everything.

I tell Pete that finding a friend is even better
than flying around the world.

In Kathmandu, a tear swells in Kitty's eye.

She stares at the stars and imagines flying
around the world with Pete …

In New Zealand they'd ski down the slopes of the Southern Alps.

In Hawaii they'd surf the wild waves at Waikiki beach.

In Scotland they'd row a boat on Loch Ness
and look out for "Nessie."

In India they'd take a long ride on Ellie the elephant.

"Just for fun," Kitty sighs.

Suddenly, there's a loud knock at her door.

It's Pete!

Kitty is flabbergasted!

He's holding the biggest bunch of chrysanthemums!

Kitty smiles just like Mona Lisa.

Pete snorts,

"I don't give two oinks if you can't fly. I like you just the way you are — Kitty from Kathmandu!"